L.T. GRUNDY

Trapped by The Blood

First edition

This book was professionally typeset on Reedsy.
Find out more at reedsy.com

Contents

Subscribe Now For Exclusive Content!

Stay In Touch With LT To Receive Book Updates and Offers!

Sign up for my newsletter HERE
You can also join our ARC team HERE

Get in touch with L.T. by email at LTGrundyBooks@gmail.com

Subscribe now for exclusive updates, promos, giveaways, and updates on the next book!

1

One

It was like riding a bicycle in the middle of winter, he had no control over what was going to happen next. The gun was a throwback to a different time and place where he was a lowly grunt doing the work of those that didn't want to get their hands dirty. He learned to separate his personal life from his business but he was cocky to think that he could have it all on a silver platter without any of the consequences.

His life before manipulating the markets wasn't for those with a weak stomach. The benefit of recruitment gave him the opportunity to travel extensively across the globe in his youth. He wasn't aware at the time how one foreign country could bleed into another until he couldn't remember where he was at any given time.

Having people in his employment to work outside conventional law made his life easier. Becoming beholden to a young man with a chip on his shoulder wasn't what he thought he would be doing in his twilight years. He didn't want to think of where he would be without a hand from the right people at the right time.

Driving was a chore he had no use for when money spoke volumes. This was the first time he wanted to be behind the wheel with the power underneath his foot.

He was dressed like any other businessman walking to and from work but, his was a story vastly different than those punching in.

They were sheep under the thumb of society to make that money before the government would sweep in to take their portion of their hard-earned dollars. The plan was simple, and it demanded swift and immediate action. He thought he could pay back his debt in full. He was mistaken.

Careless wasn't in his vocabulary.

He prided himself on knowing his adversaries and their weaknesses. It made it easier to attack them when they were vulnerable. He abhorred those that were trapped in loveless marriages going through the motions because of the children. He hated the next generation for being lazy and complacent controlled by technology.

He walked into a brick building. It was nothing out of the ordinary by outside appearances. On the surface, it was an insurance company, but what was behind closed doors had the fate of the free world in the palm of their hands.

No expense was necessary to spruce up the place. It was plain and ordinary like many other offices. There was a receptionist with her flotation devices coming into the room before her. It was a bit sexist. She was that sexual component to keep people calm when their tempers were flaring.

"I have an early morning meeting with Mr. Crosby. You can tell him his old friend, Niles Winthrop is waiting for him and I don't have all day. Pick up the phone and call him before I lose my patience and walk out of here. What you do next is the difference between a million dollar contract and the unemployment line." His persona was one that had disappeared two decades ago without a trace, presumably killed in a car accident.

Megan could see this man was serious and decided to take his request on face value. Mr. Crosby was the president. Nobody talked to him and the most they would get in greeting was a dismissive nod or grunt of reply.

She picked up the phone and hit the right extension.

"I'm sorry to bother you during your morning routine. There's a Niles Winthrop to see you. Blond hair, fairly good looking about 6 feet tall, 170 pounds with green eyes and this tiny little nondescript scar above his right eye." Describing him was a pleasure and invoked a serious need to jump into his lap until they were both satisfied beyond words.

Mr. Rhodes wasn't going to wait around forever and decided to storm by the reception desk to the elevators beyond. He heard her incessant squeaking flustered and looking for some kind of authority to insert into a tenuous situation.

"He told me to tell you to go straight up to the 10th floor and immediately take a right off the elevator until you reach the door with his name on it. I've never heard him stutter and whatever business you have with him has made him nervous. I shouldn't tell you this." She looked around, "He has a discreet exit in his office to avoid unnecessary confrontation. It leads down a set of stairs to the back of the building." She wanted to tell him her deepest darkest secrets including her kinky perversion for wearing leather masks in the bedroom.

"I appreciate the heads up and maybe I can do you a favor. Take this card and call it at your own discretion. I can see through the windows of the soul. I admire the restraint to wear clothing in public when what you want most of all is to be naked on your knees servicing many men. This one phone call will have you doing that with several well endowed black men. This is going to open a door that you can't close once it's opened." He could already see the twinkle of interest in her eyes and there was no way she was going to deny herself the chance to extinguish the fire inside of her burning out of control.

"Are you...you...going to be there?" She blurted out without thinking, grabbing onto his muscular form with a sigh of resignation.

"Sadly, I have pressing business elsewhere but I will hear all about it. They might even take some video so that I can enjoy your performance in the safety and privacy of my bedroom. If I'm impressed then you might get a phone call from me in the middle of the night. It depends on what their assessment is when they're done with you." He enjoyed the shock value of seeing her eyes light up like the Fourth of July.

"I will do whatever they say and more just to get your attention. I feel like being a dirty girl on my knees begging for them to use me for their pleasure. You will be very pleased." She had never said something so filthy in her life but it was freeing to be open and honest.

He stopped momentarily to touch her lips and watch with bated breath as she sucked the tip of his finger in this salacious way to send signals to a certain part of his anatomy. The grunt of animalistic need was followed by a hard swallow with unseemly thoughts. It revolved around her taking whatever was offered no matter how degrading.

"I will be the judge of that. The one thing you don't want to do is disappoint me. I can be very kind but can also be unforgiving when it comes to making sure you don't have a place to stay. I can rip your world apart with one phone call and have you begging on the streets for scraps." He plucked his finger from her mouth with those crimson lips telling him a story of naughty persuasion without saying a word.

He walked with long strides of confidence while thinking about the road he had put her on. His business associates would have fun with fresh meat. They were always looking for female conquests with porcelain skin and bodies that didn't quit.

It was wrong to corrupt her yet she seemed eager and willing to learn at the feet of the masters. She could easily be on the fast track to success requiring a few hours a week on her back looking up at the ceiling.

"Have the car pulled around back. I will be there shortly. Make sure nobody leaves the building without passing you. This is a matter of some urgency." He already had the blueprints of the building memorized and knew exactly where to go to find the exit.

His voice was hypnotic to those of the opposite sex. He could turn it off and on like a light switch. It was a gift and a curse. Women flocked to him when he was emanating that sexual charisma. He didn't have a shortage of young impressionable girls from the ages of 18 to 55 climbing all over him. It didn't matter if they were married, engaged, or seeing somebody seriously.

His many conquests were his outlet when he was suffering from insomnia. It was a byproduct of his training and most with his kind of expertise when it came to shooting had the same problem. Shooting someone was cold and impersonal but he learned to take enjoyment from that moment he could see their lust for life about to be extinguished.

The balancing act wasn't easy. Years of service had cost him a piece of his soul. It was gone and there was no retrieving it which meant he was capable of some heinous acts without a conscience to back them up. Stripping away what made him human had given him a license to play by a different set of rules than everybody else.

Making money was where he excelled.

"Why are you leaving so soon, Mr. Crosby? Is it something I said?" The man in front of him stopped cold and was shaking like a leaf unable to say one single word of reply.

"You should be dead. I haven't heard that name in years. I was hoping never to hear it again. Just tell me what you want," He said belligerently attempting to show a backbone to a man that scared the living daylights out of him.

Niles was the reason he went prematurely gray and bald before he was 40. There was no doubt his medical history could be attributed to Niles playing with his life like somebody did a puppet on a string.

"Don't stand there and tell me you haven't benefited from my influence in your life. You wouldn't have that trophy wife, the million dollar home on a lake in Tahoe, or the three little rug rats nipping at your ankle without me. I gave it all to you and all you had to do was give me your undying fealty. I'm not heartless. I'm not going to ask you to kill anybody." Mr. Rhodes was enjoying the way this man was sniveling like a coward with his hands holding onto the wall in fear that he was going to crumple to his knees.

"Don't beat around the bush. Twenty years and I was just starting to think I didn't have a shadow with you whispering into my ear. My therapist told me I was paranoid and gave me medication. I will do whatever you want," He complied with his request before even hearing what it was.

"I need you to put that big brain of yours to work. Do this for me and the slate is clean between us. This photograph has been digitally altered using a program to make her look different. Hair color and eye color can be changed. The one thing most people are not aware of is how they walk. It's a signature and hard to control when you are preoccupied with doing something else. This video accompanying the photographs will give you a baseline to work with." He handed him the portfolio with the CD-ROM inside taped to the back of the folder.

It was an ordinary brown folder seen in many offices.

"I will set things into motion on your behalf. I guess I should have known better to think I could run from you. Nobody is safe when you're prowling the streets looking for victims. I'm sorry to make it sound like you are some kind of monster but I wouldn't wish meeting you in a dark alley to any of my enemies." Niles didn't bother to turn around and had no interest to become an unwitting witness to his current appearance.

"There's a telephone number you can call when you have the answers I'm looking for. I'm expecting a margin for error. There will be some red herrings before we get a match. I'm going to stress keeping this secret at the risk of incurring my wrath. Nobody is to know what you're doing off the books." Mr. Rhodes had the knife ready to plunge into his back on the slim possibility he would refuse to take him seriously.

It would've been nice to taste that metaphorical blood in his mouth. Every kill in the old days came with it that bitter copper taste in his mouth. He could feed on that moment between life and death. It was a drug, something he had kicked several years earlier but, it was always in the back of his mind waiting to crawl out of the deepest part of his psyche.

He walked out whistling before climbing into the car waiting for him with tinted windows. Breathing a sigh of relief wasn't necessary. The ball was in motion and it was just a matter of time before he would know her destination. She thought hiding from the consequences to her actions was a good idea. He was on par to be one of the best in the business when it came to becoming a sniper.

Her competence in this arena had made him crave the day they would come to blows. Pitting his skills against hers would be the challenge he had been looking for. He thought they were destined to be denied the spirit of competition. Hanging up his unique skill set was the hardest thing he had ever done in his life.

He looked out the window and placed his finger on the glass pointing to Quinn in the somewhere in the distance waiting for his brand of justice.

2

Two

It was pelting rain with the threat of changing over to snow courtesy of the weatherman spouting a litany of phrases, including mentioning something about a nor'easter bearing down on the state of Maine.

"Disgruntled" and "a loner" would describe several of the patrons eating the food and drinking their coffee at the counter. The diner was right off the highway, the perfect location for travelers and drifters. The food was common everyday fare, including meatloaf and hamburgers with a special sauce to whet their appetite for dessert.

The waitress with her name tag "Marilyn" stenciled in red over her right breast was playing to the crowd. Her smile was disarming and she used her southern drawl to keep them on their best behavior. Flirting and teasing came with the job but they knew how far to push her before she was going to push back.

She was young enough to have fun but old enough to understand how her body language could be perceived. Wearing no bra was a good way to garner those tips to fend off the wolves. The academics of a pyramid scheme were simple. She would pay one bill and promise to pay another but she was never ahead of the game.

Truck drivers had come out of the inclement weather to feed their need for caffeine and food. It was a waiting game and there was no reason to be on the road unless you had a death wish. The mixture was turning the street into a slushy mess, treacherous and quite impassable unless you were willing to take your life into the palm of your hand.

Most were complacent and would eat heartily before returning to their trucks to sleep. Some would brave the elements while others had more to live for than to have their loved ones mourn their loss. It was all about the balance of work and personal life.

Nobody noticed the two tourists in the back booth eating their meals and drinking their black coffee without cream or sugar. The red leather of the seat was fading and cracking in places courtesy of father time.

There was a jukebox on every table playing old favorites from the 1980s including Lover Boy and ACDC. It was a good mixture of some of the best the industry had ever seen. Kansas was their selection with 'Carry on my wayward son' droning on in the background while they were enjoying their morning routine.

Quinn was dressed in a denim shirt and white t-shirt underneath. Lying behind her was a white parka to ward off the chill of the elements. Maine could be cruel when it came to the weather and she had learned to be prepared like the locals.

She was eating the special of the day. It was her nod of approval to the chef behind the scenes slaving over a hot stove. They never laid eyes on one another but there was mutual respect when she ordered what the chef referred to as a culinary delight.

This time it was banana bread French toast with a strawberry sauce and syrup dripping down the sides. In an instant, she was smiling despite being declared dead to the rest of the world. Agencies were no longer looking for her in the conventional sense. It didn't surprise her to learn through back channels some were not convinced of her demise. It required her to blend into her surroundings including changing her hairstyle and color every few days.

"You know what I'm going to say. We've both been thinking about it for the last couple of days and don't think I haven't noticed you looking at the map. We can't stay here. It's been a month playing tourist and claiming we are on sabbatical from a Chicago university. We need to keep the wind at our back at all times," Bryce mentioned without coming up for air only stopping momentarily to say what was on his mind before returning to his scrumptious omelet.

The eggs were flaky with a medley of different vegetables including mushrooms and onions. There was an abundance of sausage and ham with every bite. It was a meal fit for a king. The fare was simple and the price was reasonable. It was the reason why it was standing room only on a Sunday morning.

Families' had come in from the cold on their way to church to find sustenance. Young children dressed in their best were fussing and pulling at their clothes. The parents chastised and whispered about how they would be punished if they didn't behave.

"I have been thinking, it's time to move on. Somebody has to pay for making my life a living hell and taking away the only normal I've ever had. Running hasn't been the answer and maybe it's time to send a message." She took a hold of her coffee cup and drained the last of its contents before the waitress came over to refill it.

"What exactly do you have in mind? I ask already knowing I'm going to regret it." Bryce listened to the music and it was a throwback to a different era.

"My old stomping grounds have several branches in different cities. They don't advertise hiding behind shell companies like insurance and lawyers. I would like to get in touch with one of my old colleagues and have a frank discussion about how my death was prematurely reported. He's not one for surprises." Quinn thought about what had transpired over the last few days.

"It would be risky to announce you are alive. The authorities will converge and there will be nothing we can do about it. I don't like the idea of you being hunted all over again. I do feel better qualified to fight back with what you have taught me. I know I haven't been a good student and I apologize for any discomfort I've caused you," He said still feeling the bruises and bumps from sparring with her every morning without fail at the crack of dawn.

Their room in the bed and breakfast was on the main floor. The kitchen was open for their use but they had to supply the food. There was a market within walking distance and they had perused several vendors choosing fresh over frozen at the supermarket.

"You don't understand and maybe I should clarify," She said with him nodding his consent. "I want to use code words and phrases from back in the day. Those who I have worked with in the past will understand what it means while everybody else remains oblivious. I'm guessing Mr. Rhodes and whoever he is working for has a network of spies doing their bidding. I'm sure some roads meet up with others in my past. This way we can control the flood of information and be ready for the next attack by going on the offensive." It wasn't something she was looking forward to but it was better than being three steps behind waiting for the shadows to swallow them whole.

"It still sounds dangerous to me. I don't have a better idea. This weather is going to make traveling impossible for the next twenty-four hours. We may as well enjoy whatever time we have left. Let's finish here and go back to our room. I'm sure we can find other ways to amuse ourselves until this storm passes," He teased with his fingers lingering on the back of hers thinking of the many ways he could make her squeal in less than an hour.

"You have a dirty mind. It takes one to know one. Unfortunately, I took the liberty of arranging a flight out of here and we need to be at the Airport in less than twenty minutes. Whatever you have in mind is going to have to wait until we land in Boston." She was checking the flights with many being delayed but the one scheduled to depart for Boston was on time.

"I'm seriously going to miss this place. I love getting up at midnight and cooking. It alleviates my stress although, there are much more pleasurable ways to do that. We have an insatiable appetite which has nothing to do with food. I feel drained every day and I couldn't be happier," Bryce beamed with this glowing light of satisfaction in his eyes.

"You have this funny way of keeping things fresh. I don't know where you come up with the ideas but I have heard the Internet is quite knowledgeable on this subject," She hinted about finding the book underneath the mattress without coming out and admitting she was snooping.

He had compiled a list of different sexual acts including some old favorites. Some could only be performed by men and women in the prime of their life. Agility and flexibility went hand in hand. Some depictions she had found on the Internet made her stand up and salute with a woman's erection.

"I had no self-worth and I lost the will to live until I found you. This is not false platitudes. Everything I say is coming from my heart. I'm taking everything I have and I'm laying it at your feet. I was never able to feel a thing until you awakened something inside of me. I don't want to fall short when I'm trying to tell you how I feel. I watch you sleeping to make me feel that peace when everything around me is chaotic." Bryce was never much for sentimental drivel and this was a departure from his other relationships.

"I hope, it goes without saying, I feel the same way about you. Everything has changed for me and I no longer feel alone. I thought nobody could love me when I couldn't even look in the mirror and respect the person looking back at me. I don't cringe anymore when I see myself. Something has softened and I attribute it to you being in my life. It's bizarre to think of how much you have given me in such a short time." Though she still thought about the way he had betrayed her by using her brother against her.

It was cute the way he was trying to come up with unique ways to apologize. A bouquet of roses and simple gestures like love notes on the mirror when she was getting ready in the morning had become a common occurrence. She didn't want to admit how it touched her deeply to feel his affection in more than words.

Their love life was in a league of its own. They could go for hours with a few breathers in between to catch their breath. They were able to keep each other safe and warm from the intrusions of life. Sometimes they would reach out when they felt like they were drowning and the other would be there to throw them a lifeline to help them keep their head above the water.

"I've never been much for the sappy stuff. I think you deserve to be treated like a queen. There might be stormy weather but it's sunny all year around when you are standing next to me. Rescuing you has been my privilege and pleasure. Having you there to pull me from the fire literally and figuratively has shown me there is goodness in this world. I lost sight of what was important," He admitted but choked on the words feeling lighter for saying what was on his mind.

"I look back at the woman I was and I never want to see her again. This is a new evolution and I have shed the skin of my alter ego like a snake. It does come with some pitfalls like weighing the pros and cons of my actions. I have grown a conscience of faith. This gift of the silver cross around my neck reminds me of what I'm fighting for," She got up and gathered the dishes in one hand while carrying the check with the other.

"I see the world differently, no longer in black and white. There are many shades of gray." He put on his dark winter jacket with a furry hood.

The bell at the front of the door made everybody turn curious to see what fool had ventured out.

"This is a holdup! I want everybody to shut up and do what they are told.Give us what we want and there won't be any trouble." Two men walked in brandishing small revolvers with enough punching power to kill anybody that was going to show resistance.

3

Three

He was the leader, and a growing force of influence to make others follow him. Convincing his younger brother to stop during their road trip to rob a diner took very little effort. The weather was nothing when they were driving a four-wheel drive jeep, able to navigate the tough terrain of any environment. It was stolen from Canada in a little place called St. Stephen. It was just on the border and nobody was going to notice it was missing from a long-term parking facility for at least a week.

Some of the men in the diner wanted to play hero, with one quickly standing before being shot in the stomach. He dropped to his knees holding his beer gut. It sent a message to the others. They witnessed the agony of defeat up close and personal.

"I'm not fooling around here. Put all of your money and valuables into the bag my brother is quite gracious to provide. This man made the mistake of thinking that I wouldn't pull the trigger. I think I have proven how far I'm willing to go. We don't have to be enemies. Money and your valuables can be replaced. Your lives are more important than material objects. Call this an intervention for all those people living in the lap of luxury while others suffer indignities living in their purgatory underneath your nose." Jimmy Dennis was always getting into trouble, coming face to face with the law several times spending days and even weeks behind bars.

His little brother Timothy was following in his brother's footsteps. He admired his strength and willingness to go outside of his comfort zone. Losing their father made it necessary for them to stand with one another. Family was their bond even though Timothy wanted something better instead of becoming a person's worst nightmare.

His shaggy dark hair covered his eyes. He was wearing a checkered plaid red and black shirt buttoned to the top. The jacket was from the army surplus store, something soldiers wore when they faced their worst fear. It made him feel close to the action without being there. He could never tell his brother about his dream of serving his country with distinction and honor.

Quinn was watching this display and leaped soundlessly over the booth to the other side until she was on her hands and knees sneaking up from behind. Bryce didn't have a chance to say anything to her when her actions were going to speak louder than words. It was in her DNA to face overwhelming odds and destroy the myth of somebody becoming powerful just by holding a gun.

The patrons cooperated and glared with daggers the entire time. Wallets and watches followed fistfuls of cash including bank cards and credit cards. Most would be useless and would be reported stolen the moment they walked out of those doors.

"I crave a different life where I have people catering to my every whim. We didn't come from money. Most of you fight for everything you have. That should impress me but it doesn't. You are as much a part of the problem as anybody else. This gives me a different kind of buzz instead of drinking myself into a stupor." Jimmy loved the adrenaline rush of making people fear him groveling on their hands and knees to live another day.

"Take what you want and leave. This is all we have in the registers. There's over $1000. I hope you choke on it." Nicholas was the chef but nobody knew he was also the owner, not even his waitress Marilyn.

"You think you are brave by standing up to me like this. I have a good mind to put one between your eyes to end your misery. I want you to beg me for your life. It's the only way you're going to stop one of these fine people from losing their lives right in front of you. If you want to be the big man then you have to wear the big boy pants," Jimmy encouraged with his gun pressed to a young mother having breakfast with her two kids.

"My brother is trying to be fair and considerate. The best thing for everybody is to say as little as possible. There's no reason any more blood has to be shed here today. Don't try anything funny. What is it that you don't understand about that statement? Nobody deserves to go out like that," Timothy referred to the man struggling to breathe on the floor with a pool of blood surrounding him.

Marilyn was using her hands to provide pressure to the wound. It was seeping through her fingers and she was feeling faint with the fear of losing her life in the back of her mind. She didn't say a word and was waiting for it to be over.

Timothy felt a tug on his leg and he was taken out from underneath his feet until he was subdued in a chokehold. It was subtle and quite sudden without a fair warning. Timothy made the mistake of walking down along the tables in the back looking for stragglers hiding in plain sight.

What he found was Quinn waiting for the right time to strike.

Quinn held him firmly, making sure he had no way to cry out. His communication was a few indistinct wheezes and an errant slap of his hand against the black and white tile on the floor. The struggle to remain conscious had been lost. He lay there vulnerable looking like a little boy in over his head.

There was a part of Quinn that pitied him. He was a product of his environment where his brother was calling all the shots.

The older sibling thought he had all the answers. He didn't even know how to hold a gun properly. There was a familiar cut in the crease between his thumb and forefinger. It was bleeding but nothing serious. He probably didn't feel it with whatever drug was running upstream through his veins. The bravery and encouragement to do something stupid came from illegal substances.

"Please don't kill me... I have a wife and family waiting for me at home. There's too much I haven't done. My life is incomplete. There's a whole world out there to explore. What the hell am I saying? I have no wife or children. This is what I do and I enjoy cooking more than anything in this world. This place gives me the chance to delve deep into my culinary experience. I don't want to die simply because life is for the living." The chef was thinking about Marilyn and how best to approach her but too afraid to make the first move out of fear of rejection.

He had no idea Marilyn felt the same way coming from the old school of thinking where the guy had to do the asking. She was under the mistaken impression he wasn't interested.

"Passion like that doesn't come around often and you should hold onto it. My brother thinks I don't know about his extracurricular activities. I don't want to live alone. It's selfish to ask him to stick around for me. Just stop talking. I don't have the time or the inclination to think what I'm doing is wrong." Jimmy was staring at the mother and watching her remain strong for her children was an inspiration.

He backed away still holding the gun outstretched with his arm locked.

"You keep holding the gun like that and you're going to hurt yourself." Her words made him turn unexpectedly where she was able to twist and break his grip on the trigger.

The gun landed squarely in her hands turning the tables to make this young punk stare at her in shock and confusion.

He began shaking uncontrollably with tremors all over his body. Jimmy dropped to his hands and knees with his hands in a prayer formation. Before he uttered a single word to plead for his life he was unconscious at her feet with a bit of his blood sticking to the handle of the revolver.

"I have never seen anybody move that fast. The meal is on the house. You have a standing invitation to come back here anytime. Your money is no good here. I will call the police. It's going to take them some time to get out here due to the weather." The chef stood back up and was rewarded with a kiss from Marilyn to make his mind muddled by the impromptu affection she was showing him.

Quinn took him aside so they could talk in private away from those mumbling underneath their breath. They were astonished and quite taken back by her act of bravery.

"I would rather somebody else take responsibility for this. Pick somebody at random. I really don't care. You are a leader even if you don't think so. Don't worry about Marilyn, she already harbors an interest beyond your love of food. We both know this is your place. Don't look surprised. I will keep your secret but you have to promise to keep my involvement in this quiet. Nobody needs to know. Give them a free meal and they will tell the police whatever you want them to." Quinn looked down at the two assailants both restrained with telephone cords and belts.

"I'm guessing you are running from something. Whatever it is they have no idea what they are facing. I see things with a laser focus. My heart was beating out of my chest the entire time they were waving that gun around. You didn't even blink an eye. I had the same ice water running through my veins when I was serving my country. It seems like yesterday." The chef had the night terrors and he never took one moment for granted except when it came to his personal life.

They stared at one another for quite some time recognizing the soldier in each other. He was learning to adjust to civilian life outside of the scope of the military. He was proud to serve but was grateful to come home alive when others didn't have that same luck.

"This is your place of business. I'm not sure why you feel it's necessary to keep the information private. You have your reasons. It's precisely the way I feel about my privacy. I'm no longer running away from something. I'm running toward something but I'm going to need a head start. They can't know I'm coming for them until it's too late. Keep my name out of the report." She was about to walk away when she noticed Timothy stirring looking around amazed and then resigned to his fate.

She walked over and knelt by his side taking him by the hair to look more menacing than she was.

"I'm willing to let you go but only if you live your dreams without your brother taking away your future. The military will mold you and turn you into a man. Don't lose the innocence. That's the mistake I made and maybe I can stop you from making the same one." She had to wait to see him staring blindly at her until finally the truth was written all over his face.

"He's in my blood and I can't shake him. What kind of brother would I be to leave him here to face the long arm of the law? I would die a little more each day realizing I was free when he was behind bars living a life of abject failure." Timothy was quite articulate and wasn't afraid to throw around the big words when his mind was going a million miles an hour.

"Listen to her and maybe you can eke out your own path. I will survive inside. Do what you've always wanted to. Join up and see the world. I can't begrudge you the chance to make something out of your life. Just promise me not to forget where you came from," Jimmy beseeched and felt it was necessary to give him his freedom before the only future would be a pine box or twenty years in prison.

Quinn grinned knowingly and untied Timothy with the blessing of the patrons. They could tell his heart wasn't into it and decided to give him a second chance.

"That was probably the first selfless act you have ever committed in your life. There's hope for you but it's not going to be simple. There are programs inside to become a productive member of society when you are released. Become versed in those programs and read a book every week. It doesn't matter the topic. That sense of accomplishment will give you the tools to weather whatever this life will throw at you." She slapped his face lightly in a mocking gesture and received a sneer of derision in return.

Quinn was right about the free meal. It was the glue to make their stories stick together. Unfortunately, one of the patrons took a video and had it on the cloud for the whole world to see.

The wheels were in motion and Quinn didn't have to visit her friend to make the enemy come looking for her.

4

Four

It was a week later when they finally walked into the sacred halls of a black site. It seemed relatively normal. The outside appearance was a coffee shop with custom made brews with a variety of different names. Those serving the customers had knowledge and expertise when it came to performing feats of amazing artistry in the cup.

The musical melody of the machines running at tip-top efficiency was white noise to most waiting for their order. Quinn loved the sound the machines made and the smell of coffee.

They had no idea what was beyond the doors down a flight of stairs into the belly of the beast.

Quinn made her way down the hallway leading to the bathroom. She produced a gold key card. She was quite aware the card access might be revoked. She was counting on the bureaucracy to be lax in certain departments concentrating on terrorist threats and high-level targets of interest.

The awkward silence was a heart-stopping ordeal. It finally clicked with the sliding door of an elevator opening in front of her. It was stainless steel with a variety of buttons that lit up in red every time somebody touched one. She climbed into the self-imposed prison of a four by eight coffin. She was never comfortable in elevators where they could plummet to the ground below at remarkable speeds leaving the occupant screaming all the way down.

Bryce was going to be understandably upset when he woke up to find she was missing. Exhausting him wasn't easy. She had him running ragged from store to store. It was a good way to make him fall into a deep slumber before supper.

This time was the sweet spot when those 9 to 5 workers were making their way home. Depending on their status they could be greeted by a fur baby, a child screaming for attention, or a TV dinner stacked with others in the freezer in a variety of meal choices. It was a convenience but a lonely existence when you pulled back the plastic to see the steam rising.

The door opened and a young woman in a striped pant suit got in carrying a briefcase. She was small in stature with a huge voice. She was talking quite loudly using the portion of her blue tooth connected to her phone to multitask with her fingers surfing the Internet for a place to stay for the evening.

"I'm telling you these people have no idea what they're doing. My audit confirms they have been working well beyond their budget for years. There is some serious cost-cutting to do in this department. I know it's not going to be a favorable option. That extra funding can go to school systems and homeless shelters." Abigail Masters loved her job and was quite detail-oriented with several things happening at the same time.

Quinn stayed quiet watching and listening like a fly on the wall. This girl was ill-equipped to understand the agency's protocol. She saw things in black and white watching where the money was trickling down without having any idea of the hardships agents had to endure.

"I'm not here to make friends. Popularity has never been something I have concerned myself with. My mandate is clear. I have to find a way to cut costs by $50,000,000. This will be half of that mark. I can always find other sources of income that don't involve the government's spending." She was well put together, prim and proper with an air of sophistication, courtesy of the way that she was dressed to impress.

Quinn had so much to say and didn't even know where to begin. The risk was too great for discovery and she had to remain steadfast with her tongue squarely in her mouth.

Sharing was never her strong suit, but this love on the run was getting ridiculous.

There was one person inside the stronghold where a rogue faction of the CIA was running rampant without restrictions. Only a select few within the government knew of its existence including the president of the United States.

He had sent Miss Masters on a fool's errand. Election year was fast approaching and he needed a platform to puff his chest to the masses. The man was not well-liked and the possibility of losing out on a second term was making him nervous.

"This is going to be my recommendation. He listens to me. I know what needs to be done and I'm not afraid of saying what is on my mind without filtering the nonsense of being politically correct. I give him the math and it always adds up." Abigail had become aware of somebody standing in the corner out of the corner of her eye.

Quinn had never come home to a hero's welcome with the ticker-tape parade. People didn't know what she did and they would probably be disgusted by the senseless act of one shot changing the course of history. In that moment when it was the perfect silence to make everything as clear as day was where she lived in perfect harmony.

There was no further discussion and the phone went dead.

"I really wish you hadn't heard any of that. I'm going to have to threaten you with litigation. Say one word to anybody and I will be forced to bring you up on charges." She turned and faced the person eavesdropping on her conversation.

Her green eyes conveyed recognition beyond the casual glance. Her lips suddenly became dry and her tongue was thick in her mouth. Her legs wanted to move but they were frozen in place unable to take a step. The woman wasn't built for combat and her training was in the classroom and not on the field of battle.

"I wasn't expecting to be discovered. You must have a photographic memory. It's too bad you couldn't leave well enough alone. I wasn't happy with what you were saying but I didn't interfere. I see you're not going to afford me the same courtesy. It's interesting when you are petrified staring at the face of evil." She easily disarmed her of one weapon and her phone before striking her so hard with the back of her hand that her head bounced off the elevator.

She grunted and groaned with her vision blurred until she was on the floor gasping for air. She had a splitting headache and wasn't able to say anything beyond the gibberish coming out of her mouth. It sounded like she had a stroke. The shock of being hit with callous disregard was a blow to her fragile ego.

Stunned was an understatement.

Abigail clawed at her ankle where she found a knife strapped in a leather pouch. It could be easily accessed by bending slightly at the waist in a flirting gesture that would become deadly.

"I would be doing everybody a favor if I were to kill you. That report you hold so dear would never see the light of day. It's a good thing I have grown as a person over the last couple of months. If this had happened when I was still the same person then you wouldn't have a hope in hell of surviving outside of this elevator." She did the same thing to her as other victims including the two young punks back at the diner.

One brother was in police custody and the other was recruited into the Marines to learn discipline and find a purpose. He had the chance to turn his life around at the expense of his older brother. Quinn had done something on his behalf to have somebody reach out to him inside to give him the one chance for intellectual pursuit.

"I need... I need to tell somebody," Abigail squeaked with her body going slack until she was asleep.

The elevator opened on a skeleton crew with the lights dimmed. They were busy typing madly on the computer and going over a wide array of communiqués from across the world. They didn't see how Quinn was dragging her overpowered opponent down the hall into a janitor's closet.

She broke the lock making it impossible for somebody to get inside without the tools of the trade. It was a temporary solution. She had to get in and out without anybody seeing her and raising the alarm.

The door she was looking for was at the end of the hall. His name was a slap to her face. She couldn't believe how he had treated her. Breaking his hand was the least of his concerns. The brass stopped her from breaking every bone in his body one at a time. She promised to come back seething with rage with her teeth bared like a ferocious animal on the prowl.

He was usually high on the mountain with the bigwigs on the tenth floor of a high-rise with an insurance company as the legitimate business to shield them from the public and foreign interests. This would be his way of slumming it but he was always arrogant about teaching the recruits something they couldn't find in the classroom. Young women had become his victim but she had been watching diligently to see if he was taking her threat seriously.

Mr. Evan Crosby wasn't much of a man. He looked like one, but he was taught to see women as sexual objects to be conquered.

The door was open a crack and he was at his desk in the trenches.

She walked in disturbing nothing until she was underneath his desk having a bit of fun at his expense. It was to make sure he wasn't able to run but also to teach him a lesson about manners when it came to women. She wanted him to know the glass ceilings were breaking. Improper behavior would no longer be tolerated in the workplace including government positions.

She made her presence known by standing in his shadow next to his chair.

"Jesus Christ, you gave me a start and maybe you should learn to knock before you enter. I don't have time to hold your hand on every single detail." He was perturbed and knew from the feminine scent this girl wasn't familiar.

"I've never needed you to hold my hand for anything. You are a pencil-pushing, know nothing, dick-less wonder. I can't see how any woman would give you the time of day. You can fool them some of the time but your true face always reveals itself." She moved a little closer with her hands on his shoulders to feel him cringe at her voice.

"It's not really you...if I don't see your face. Coming here was the worst mistake of your life. There's no way you're going to get out of here alive. I wanted to believe you were finally gone. That one time where you faked your death and suddenly emerged out of the shadows into the light was one for the record book." He was talking fast but he was also thinking about ways to communicate to the outside office without her knowledge.

"I have taken everything into account. I walked in here knowing every single detail about this place. Imagine my surprise when my card key accessed this place. There's something in the way that you look at me. It would be so easy to snap your neck with one jerking motion. I think I would find more pleasure in letting you feel my hot breath on your neck every single day of your life. The bullet with your name on it dances in the palm of my hand every night before I go to bed. You are a man of habit and routine." She had mapped his daily life from the time he picked up his copy of the newspaper to when he disappeared behind closed doors with a comely young blonde that wasn't his wife.

"I don't know what you were thinking coming here," He stuttered with his hands in plain sight afraid to make any wrong move.

"I have these incriminating photographs. I've been waiting for the right time to use them against you to make you compliant. This is you doing obscene things to this young lady for an hour every Thursday. I'm sure your wife would love to hear about your afternoon delights. It's not an idle threat when she holds the purse strings." She knew his money was nothing without her by his side smiling sweetly to the public.

"What do you want?" This wasn't the first time he had said this and it wasn't going to be the last.

"I want you to circulate this..." She stopped and stared at the computer.

There was a video of her taking control of the scene with the speed of a Bengal tiger poised to jump an unsuspecting victim in the diner. The movements were her signature.

"It looks like word has already gotten out. I was hoping for a little more discretion. Do you want to tell me what this is about?" There was another video playing side by side a little grainy but still her when you looked at it closely.

"I got a request a few days ago to look for you. I've been combing through every little bit of information. I finally found this moment before you walked into my office. You should be more careful about attracting the wrong kind of attention." He got up quickly and ran for the door only to trip over his shoelaces falling flat on his face chipping one of his teeth.

He turned laughing while pressing a small button at the bottom at the threshold of the door. The building locked down with the doors swinging shut automatically clicking into place.

"You're trapped. Mr. Winthrop is coming personally. I do believe he wrote the book on strategies. Everything you learned came from his unique experience. He knows everything you know but you don't know everything he knows. Let the games commence where only one of you will survive. Personally, I would love both of you to take each other out at the same time." He wagged a finger and it broke with the scream in his throat, suffocated by the pain radiating through his limb.

She stood there after he fainted wondering how she was going to best proceed.

5

Five

It was a stroke of good fortune the moment the building locked down. Mr. Rhodes got firsthand knowledge with an alert to his phone. He was waiting down the hall going over some footage. He was using strategy to stay one step ahead.

He didn't expect her to fall right into his lap in an environment he was born into. The building was his baby and he knew every nook and cranny including the security measures. A backdoor was open to him into the computer to make good use of the weapons including cutting off the oxygen to certain rooms.

The cameras confirmed she was there but she didn't look the same. It was amazing to see her after offering her a job in his employment. That seemed like a lifetime ago when they could have been friends. Denying him her services put them on a direct course where they were going to collide with catastrophic results.

"The fly has gotten caught in my web. This is going to be fun for me. It's been some time since I have been in the field. I might have a little bit of rust to work off. I'm going to give you some incentive. You beat me and I will tell you why you are being targeted. I will even give you positive proof of the person responsible. I wouldn't get your hopes up. This building is my playground." He pressed a button after making some adjustments until her room was being deprived of oxygen.

Quinn could feel the change and tried to conserve as much oxygen as possible by breathing with shallow breaths. It was only going to work for a short time before she would succumb. The last thing she wanted was somebody watching her every move.

She quickly covered the camera with Mr. Crosby's jacket hanging by the door.

Her best bet was to get out of the room but there was no telling what was waiting on the other side. It didn't matter. Dying in a lonely room next to a man she despised was not going to be her epitaph.

Jumping from the frying pan into the fire was preferable.

She rummaged through the desk until she found a bottle of cognac. It was flammable and could easily be turned into a weapon. She had the means to light the flame but there was no accounting for the lifeblood of fire once it got started.

There was a way to turn the alcohol into the living embodiment of a bomb. She found several pills in the desk for a variety of ailments. Adding certain ones to the alcohol would cause a molecular change. It would explode with the force of a small incendiary device.

The timing was crucial. The bottle would have to leave her hand seconds before the explosion. Being oxygen-deprived was causing her head to spin and she felt like the room was moving around her while she was standing in the axis of the room.

She dragged Evan behind the desk and tipped it over to give them a modicum of defense against the blast. It was hard to justify killing him when her conscience had been awakened.

"I don't know what you are doing in there but it's not going to work. Give up and maybe I will make it painless. I wouldn't count on it. I think you already know how your defeat is affecting me. I want to hear you say the words before I decide to give you a momentary reprieve. It shouldn't surprise you how I am going to revel in finally putting you out of your misery. Take your time making your decision." His voice was familiar but she was distracted to understand things had come full circle.

"I'm not going to give you the satisfaction of hearing me grovel for my life. I would rather die in this room than to say the words you want to hear." She held the bottle and screwed off the top until adding a few of those pills to see the chemical reaction up close and personal.

Danger lurked beyond the doors but she was going to have to face that when the time came. She wasn't very good in school. She had learned several different topics including chemistry after walking away from the hallowed halls. It wasn't being crammed down her throat and she could concentrate without the constant belittling of her classroom mates.

The liquor was bubbling and she closed the top to make the seal complete. The chemical reaction was quite significant. She watched with careful deliberation counting down in her head until she finally had to release the bottle at the risk of getting her hand blown off.

"I would tell anybody on the other side of the door to run," She warned before throwing overhand with the bottle flying.

It exploded when the bottle hit the door square in the center. The spontaneous reaction was instantaneous.

It blew out catching two agents waiting to storm in by surprise. They had chemical burns to their faces and hands but they were thankfully too busy running around to notice her.

It was almost comical like some slapstick routine.

Quinn didn't take the chance of running into a hail of bullets.

She grabbed the closest one and used him as a human shield. There was no way to know where the gunshots were coming from. The man in front of her took the full extent of the barrage of bullets. Quinn pulled the trigger underneath his arm returning fire without seeing what she was shooting at.

There was this fleeting form and it dove behind a desk before coming back up like a game of deadly whack-a-mole. It wasn't the same kid's game and there was nothing amusing about trying to put one between his eyes. Quinn took no pleasure from using the stranger to keep breathing a little bit longer.

It was not a nice day to die.

"I'm going to have to stop thinking in a two-dimensional way when dealing with you. I thought you changed but it seems when it comes to survival anything goes. I like that about you. There's no reason to stand on ceremony. I'm trying to kill you and you're trying to do the same thing to me. There are no rules when it comes to engaging an enemy in the field of battle. It doesn't matter if it is in a foreign territory or right here at home." Mr. Rhodes was having fun jarring with his adversary hoping to get underneath her skin long enough for her to make a mistake.

The elevator was useless and would require her to hope for the best. The stairs gave her an exit strategy. He would come after her and it was exactly what she wanted. The only way to ensure that was going to happen was to goad him into pitting his skills against her.

Words could be weapons and she was very good at speaking without a filter.

"I know who you are." Those five words were said in haste.

She still hadn't come to that conclusion.

She was clearheaded and felt completely at ease ready to do what was necessary. The mind was a terrible thing to waste. She wasn't going to break easily and he would have to get his hands on her which was going to be easier said than done.

"I was wondering when it was going to dawn on you. Truth be told, I was hoping to see the look on your face when we came face to face. I don't mind telling you my identity is something I take very seriously. It's just another reason to make sure you don't have the means to say anything to anybody." It was clear one of them was going to die and he swore underneath his breath it wasn't going to be him.

"I know exactly what I need to do. Displaying your dead body to the public will send a message. There will be a shock wave, unlike anything anybody has ever seen in this business. I won't kill you until you give me the name and where I can find them. You might not think it's going to happen but I can assure you my mental acuity is up for anything you throw at me." She was still feeling the effects of the oxygen deprivation.

"Look at what you did and tell me you're one of the good guys. That line has been blurred too many times to count in this profession. I don't pretend to be some kind of saint. I thought I got away from this but maybe I was destined to step back on the same path one last time." He was leaving no stone unturned about to face his fear of going toe to toe with somebody who could match his skills in the shooting arena.

Quinn pushed the body forward and was concealed behind the fire door. This was her way of living for another day. Every second counted. If this was going to be her last day she was going to make the best of it by taking as many of them with her as possible.

"I'm not one of the good guys. Deep down there will always be that dark passenger lurking underneath the surface. I go by the beat of my own drum. Regardless of what you think of me, there is a cold-blooded killer running through the ice water in my veins," Quinn yelled through the door while checking her ammunition to see she was running low and was going to have to improvise.

She was on the side of righteousness but it came with the harsh reality of picking up the gun and using it in the most extreme way possible. Two rounds weren't going to be near enough. Her opponent had no idea what she was working with. It was an advantage she was going to take to the bank.

There was no way she could forgive her enemies without some serious soul searching. The sign mentioning there was construction above on the next floor was giving her an idea. It was time to take the fight elsewhere where no innocent civilians would be found in the crossfire. Quinn had to shake her head realizing she was thinking about others instead of her self-preservation.

"I've committed to taking you out of the game. Be prepared for the fight of your life. Killing you would be my pleasure but I can't do that. Softening you up for the kill is my job. I think everything is going according to plan." Mr. Rhodes pressed a button and the fire suppression devices went off sending down a cloud of what would feel like napalm.

Quinn covered her mouth with her sleeve and dodged several of the sprays but there was no way to avoid all of them. It did have the side effect of obscuring her from detection while she ran up the stairs two at a time. She loved every minute of it and felt bad for taking pride in her work.

She stopped and waited by the door the next floor up. Peering down into the fog created by the fire suppression units made it hard to see anything. It wasn't normal regular everyday water. No expense was spared to make sure biological weapons couldn't survive in a hostile environment.

"Come for me at your peril," Quinn urged while depending on his arrogance to make her a target worthy of his skills.

"Be careful what you wish for." Mr. Rhodes fired one short burst from his weapon before standing and delivering his verdict of guilty, playing judge, jury, and executioner.

The last one made him angry. He was going to take it out on Quinn by making sure there wasn't much left of her when he dragged her body barely breathing in front of her accuser.

Quinn pulled the door open and the spring made it come back and slam against her. She lost her grip on her gun and watched horrified when it bounced and went down an open grate. The one weapon at her disposal was no longer in her hands. These were the things that happened in the field when you had to assess the situation and come up with a reasonable facsimile of a plan.

He was coming and all she had was her environment which didn't amount to much. It was going to have to do considering the alternative was wishing for a fate where she could finally rest in peace.

6

Six

It wasn't what she was expecting and she had to take a moment to get her bearings. The construction zone was dangerous with open windows and equipment including nail guns and jackhammers. A layer of dust covered the plastic on the tables with blueprints underneath protected from the elements.

She wiped her finger across the dust and soon turned the area into a snowstorm of sawdust. The door opened and she saw the shadow of a man standing there framed in the threshold. She was creating a blanket to hide within while she found something to even the odds.

"My heart breaks for you. If it helps, your paramour isn't going to be alive for long. I sent a kill squad to handle him while I kept you occupied. You can say whatever you want but I know he means something to you. He is a liability. You already know that but you insist on bringing him into this world. Love is a useless and damning emotion." He had the gun with several others ready to bring this fight to its inevitable end.

"I know what you're trying to do. Talking me to death is something I wasn't expecting from you. Your expertise is renowned and has been talked about around the water cooler for quite some time. There's this image burning in my mind I can't seem to shake. Things are getting clearer by the second. I brought you to me but you probably think it's the other way around. It's almost laughable when you think about it." Quinn was underneath some thick plastic with a nail gun but she had to be careful about pulling the cord too tightly when it was plugged into the wall.

Mr. Rhodes was amused by the snowstorm of sawdust. He had to admire her ability to think outside the box. That trait wasn't shared by many and those who had it could say without a shadow of a doubt it came in handy.

He thought about his daily routines and how he was constantly challenging himself without a moving target. This was different and he was going to have to account for every variable when it wasn't possible.

He took a few steps with his finger on the trigger. The room was dark with several noises to attract his attention. The plastic moved and he turned to address it with a bullet only to be disappointed nobody was there.

Quinn could hear him but there was nothing she could do until he was within her line of sight. Egging him on was a good way to keep him talking but at the same time, he would be able to find her. She avoided this by moving every so often. She made sure to bring the extension cord with her wrapped around her shoulder and arm.

She couldn't stop thinking about his last comment. Bryce had learned a lot about himself. Watching him transform slowly and surely was like looking in a mirror when she was first training to be one of the best sharpshooters in the business. It took a lot of coaxing and coaching but he wasn't near as ready as he made her believe.

It was all about contending with one problem before tackling another. It was dangerous to keep those thoughts prevalent when she had this guy stalking her. His tactic of trying to make her lose her composure was something right out of her playbook.

Getting lost in a dream and not knowing where to turn was what she faced every night.

Things were going too slow and she needed more information. This man had first-hand knowledge of those practices. Waiting for some small clue to lift the fog of confusion from her eyes was taking too long.

"I can hear you breathing. Pain is going to be your motivator. I'm going to get every little bit of information out of you before turning you over. I have some questions and they are long past due for answers. I'm going to be the last page in your history." Mr. Rhodes enjoyed the hunt and the smell of fear in the air.

It was pungent with a sweet aftertaste. He had almost forgotten what it was like to play in the sandbox with those of his peers. This girl was sending messages and people were starting to take notice. It was the reason why he proffered the invitation to join him.

"I have many chapters left to go before my story is written. You are going to be a footnote, nothing more than a mention before being glossed over by my experiences. Bryce is in my life for a reason. I don't believe in love at first sight. We grew to show affection but you wouldn't know anything about that." She was constantly moving, staying three steps ahead to make her voice travel from one corner of the room to the next.

"It's a gift to know what goes on in a person's mind. I've always been a strange entity. Growing up, I was looked at as different but I was never going to fit into any social circle. I'm telling you this to give you a brief idea about the person you are facing. I hold you in high esteem which is the reason I'm honored to bring you the best challenge of your life." He did mean everything but it wasn't going to stop him from paying back a debt of honor worth 100 of her.

He did notice her voice was everywhere and had to smile by the way that she was keeping him guessing. Others wouldn't have thought to play the game in much the same way.

The tension was thick and he had the knife to cut through it into her very flesh right to the bone. The serrated edge would make her scream indicative of somebody being tortured for information.

Quinn was down on her hands and knees, giving him little chance to see her until it was too late. Patience was her friend and she could feel the cold trickle of indecision running down her spine.

The way he was talking made it sound impersonal. She took it very personally when he targeted her.

Bryce was going to have to fight overwhelming odds beyond the measure of any man. His bad dream was going to turn into a nightmare. She should have realized separating was the worst mistake of her life when they were stronger together.

Her love made it impossible to let him go. The voice of this hunter was driving her crazy nagging at her consciousness. Breathing through it was like swimming through water in the dark having nowhere to go.

His footsteps were right there holding her hostage with her breath short and her heart drumming a beat in her chest. Fear was to be embraced and not a reason to run screaming in the opposite direction. She was on a storm watch waiting for the clouds to part to see her enemy in a position to take him down.

"I understand you more than anybody, including Bryce. We come from the same train of thought. I was a few years ahead of you. It's funny they still talk about me after all these years. The record has never been beaten not even by you." His name was Niles Winthrop, but something changed him until he was looking for something better deciding on surrounding himself with money and power.

"Niles, every recruit learns about you, but you have become a ghost. They don't want to talk about how you disappeared from the landscape without a trace. I wonder what they would say if they were to learn the truth. I know there would be a lot of interest if I were to send a discreet message to make you number one with a bullet," Quinn mocked still trying to figure out the voice but knowing the past had a funny way of finding her when she least expected it.

Quinn saw him coming and waited for the count of 10 before pressing the trigger. She held it down and fired indiscriminately several large and deadly nails.

Mr. Rhodes felt the first two tear into his left knee. He jumped back in time to avoid being riddled by them. He didn't make a sound but inside he was screaming bloody murder. There was a trail of blood as he held his knee and moved to a more strategic location in the room.

"It looks like you have gotten first blood. I was getting used to being the hunter but somehow you turned the tables. I'm not going to be like everybody else you have faced in the past. Turning tail and running isn't something in my blood. I have a duty to perform and nothing is going to stop me." It did give him food for thought about the reason why she was using a nail gun instead of the weapon he had seen her with.

"That's got to hurt like hell. You got very lucky and I hope you don't forget it. Come a little closer and I'll make sure my marksmanship is better." Quinn was elated with her hand steady with those nails in abundance ready to give him more than he bargained for.

"The sweetest lie is the one we tell ourselves. I don't concern myself with pain. I can shut it off but I don't think you can do the same thing. I'm guessing you somehow lost your gun and that was probably the sound I heard before I came into the room. This is going to be fun," He fumed and began to cut off her egress one quadrant at a time.

Quinn lay down flat on her stomach holding the nail gun and watching for any movement. This was better than any drug. Self-medicating was something she tried but it did very little to quell the horrors she has seen in her nightmares.

The nail gun was inferior to her rifle with the scope to zero in on a target. These were close quarters. There was nothing like firing that one shot from a distance. Her sweet spot was putting an enemy down with that sound echoing to make her pulsate with that feeling deep down.

There was no cheer and life was better when she was under the gun. Feeling the pressure was something she thrived on. It made her feel alive with the adrenaline rushing through her veins to keep her alert honed to a razor's edge.

She inadvertently scratched her shoulder with the table she was under moving a fraction of an inch. It was something she tried to bury but there was always that nervous twitch.

The bullet ripped through the plastic like it was made of butter. She was knocked backward and lying on her back looking at the ceiling. She grabbed her shoulder to feel the sickening wetness of sticky blood seeping through her fingers. It was meant to slow her down and it was doing a remarkable job of doing just that.

"How many times have they told you during basic training to concentrate? I remember it like it was yesterday. I hated the way they tested us to see what we could handle when push came to shove. The bullet was one of many." He walked through the sawdust and felt this euphoria better than any sex.

"I live my life with no regrets. I've got my issues but he accepts me. We forget what went wrong but those moments are forever tattooed in our minds. The one thing we don't do is become cocky. That is the death knell for any soldier. Time has passed you by and you're not the same person who held that record. Take your best shot and make it a good one because you're only going to get one," She insisted with the nail gun a few feet away teasing her with the possibility of getting the upper hand.

"You know I can't resist history repeating itself. I want you to be truly afraid of what is going to happen next. I have it on good authority Bryce has already taken his last breath.

He stepped out into the opening over the top of her where he could see her reaction.

"I do believe we have some unfinished business," He clucked with an arrogance that wasn't pretty.

"Tell me about it," Quinn spoke with her teeth clenched holding back the flood of pain from escaping into an unsolicited scream of defiance.

7

Seven

Bryce walked with a purpose down the hallway stewing in his juices from being betrayed. She had left him in the middle of the night without his knowledge. That woman was incorrigible and he thought how best to chastise her for her behavior when she finally walked through those doors.

He had no idea where she went considering the black site she had talked about was in a secret location hidden from the scrutiny of the public. There was no point in lamenting over something he couldn't control. The pain of that knife twisting in his gut metaphorically speaking had him up walking around pacing the floor like a caged lion.

There was no misunderstanding. She didn't trust him to have her back when the chips were down. He thought about the morning training sessions and how she continually grilled him incessantly until he had no more energy. In retrospect, he probably shouldn't have closed his eyes but exhaustion was a byproduct of the training.

There was nothing perfect about her technique.

The one thing he did learn was to never give up. As much as he hated being knocked down, he was thrilled by the prospect of standing back up again without her help. He wasn't a polished soldier but there was potential to grow into a fighting force.

He sat down and began to take apart the gun in front of him before putting it back together again as fast as possible. He wanted to beat his record of 20 seconds and shaved off three of those seconds with a smile.

He had his own set of thoughts and it never occurred to him there was a warrior hiding within him. The motion of pulling the trigger was almost second nature without thinking about it. The room was dark with the drapes drawn and one light over the stove making shadows dance all over the walls.

He got a sudden whiff of gasoline. It was a familiar scent to make him stand up at attention with the gun in his hand. The bullets were on the table and he quickly with a steadfast approach put them into the chamber before locking the clip in place.

He couldn't understand how they found him when they had gone out of their way to scrub whatever digital footprint they made. It could've been as simple as old school by watching and waiting to see some sign of him appear on a camera somewhere. He had gone out to get supplies to clear his head after finding her missing.

They were going to smoke him out by attempting to burn him alive. He did like the smell and the heat brought him back to another time he would rather forget.

"This is where things get interesting. I can hear you. Say whatever is on your mind. One chance is all you have to convince me to stop this madness. I've been given my marching orders but I'm willing to entertain other ideas. Throw out a number and you never know what might stick. I can be bought. The one stumbling block is you don't know the number. What do you have?" This voice was coming from inside with Bryce looking around unaware there was a speaker right at the window.

"I'm not going to dignify that with a response. Any scenario is still going to get me killed. A mercenary is hired for his expertise and discretion. This is something I have learned. It was a painful lesson. I don't have the kind of money you are looking for to turn the other cheek. I doubt you would even do it as a matter of principle." He was wearing his white sleep pants with the drawstring pulled tautly.

The accompanying white shirt was open to reveal his bare chest. He had an arsenal but he was going to have to use it in the right way. Panic was starting to set in but he was determined to ignore the common sense approach of running when that was exactly what they were expecting from him.

He looked around before grabbing a blanket to smother the flames. They spread quickly and he saw no other choice. The house was in the middle of nowhere and the past was to avoid burning alive was to leave.

A deep breath was followed by Bryce walking back to the center of the room. The room couldn't be opened. Nailed shut and painted over might it was going to be the hard way.

"I'm coming out," He snickered at the connotation of the statement before running toward the window with the blanket around him.

He didn't consider it a victory when he was abandoning the weapons to level the playing field. The woods were where he knew how to live with very little besides his trusty pocket knife. His father's words came back and he was reliving his childhood.

That one summer was spent with him and his grandfather for 4 months tracking and hunting wild animals. There were other dangers and weapons that didn't include bullets. It was a treacherous terrain with jagged rocks and deep inclines turning into cliffs to take your breath away.

He didn't know anything about the surrounding area until he made a conscious effort to find out. It was similar to the cabin where two generations taught him the meaning of fighting for survival. That was the training he never talked about but it was always there waiting for the right time to come out.

The glass came at him fast and he put his shoulder into it. The velocity of his takeoff had the glass buckling under the strain. It splintered and broke with the fragments cutting into the blanket attempting to find his flesh.

He was outside and could see the forest for the trees. It was still a trek to get there and there was no telling what was waiting for them. He had the foresight to bring one gun, but it was all he could carry. Traveling light would give him room to maneuver and getting to the high ground would make the effort to sneak up on him almost impossible.

There was no point in turning to face what was coming. The ground was soon chewed up around him with the mercenaries coming for his blood.

The snow-covered grass was churning with every bullet making him dance to a different tune. He breathed deeply feeling one bullet flying by his ear. It hurt but he ignored the pain long enough to secure his freedom within the canopy of trees.

He could see where he was going and had mapped out the area from Internet sources. Taking a walk around the property gave him a better understanding. It was a precaution when everything he had seen and done up to this point had proven to him things happened when you least expected it.

"I applaud the effort but it's not going to make much of a difference. Jumping through the window was something unexpected from you. It doesn't change anything between us. I don't know you and I don't want to know you. The only thing concerning me is how many zeros are going to be on that check when I hold your head up high to my client. I hope you enjoy this moment because you're not going to get another one." Anson Stone was good at his job and his platoon wasn't chosen at random.

They were stone cold killers ready to do anything for the almighty dollar. They didn't hold regular hours like nine to five jobs. They found that adrenaline rush in battle couldn't be duplicated anywhere else. It was the reason why they gravitated toward the other side of the law where there were many gray areas.

Being declared dead or missing in action was what they had in common.

"It's getting cold outside and you might want to bundle up. I'm going to be transparent with you. The one thing you didn't want was for me to find my way out here. This is my home away from home. I can't remember the last time I have been cornered like an animal. I stand corrected. I've been in this position before too many times to count. There is truth in everything I say." Bryce wanted them to know how pointless it was for them to pursue him by using psychological warfare to get his point across.

"My comprehension of life in the wild is quite extensive. You don't have a monopoly on surviving in the elements. I'm looking forward to seeing what you have to offer as a challenge. I hope you don't take this the wrong way. I'm not expecting much. You haven't lived in the trenches like the rest of us. You don't know the hardships and what we had to do to survive. It makes me mad to hear you talk like you have some idea," Anson remembered in vivid clarity those people who had died by his hands with the blood seeping into his fingers staining them with a psychic link to the past.

He signaled his men and they fanned out to try a military tactical maneuver requiring boxing him in. There was no point in saying anything more but he was happy to play the game. His voice would help him to triangulate his location. Five men against one were odds he could live with. They were trained beyond the measure of a man to swallow down their fear in the face of any adversary.

"Before we take this too far maybe we can come to some kind of compromise. Is there anything I can do to make you turn around and go back the way you came? There's no reason not to ask the question. I won't know the answer unless I put it out there." Bryce was checking his gun to see he had 12 bullets in the clip.

There was a knife but it wasn't very sharp with several other tools including scissors and a can opener.

"I know you're not going to like hearing this. There's absolutely nothing you can say to change my mind. I'm sure you are an innocent party in all of this but it doesn't matter. The benefits of extensive training and experience are my advantage. I've hunted better than you and wear the scars to prove it. I doubt you knew what you wanted to do when you were barely in your teens. I've been doing this for over twenty years." Anson didn't like killing but the hunt was an entirely different breed of animal.

"I don't suppose it would matter if I said I had somebody special," Bryce mentioned thinking it was a last-ditch effort some kind of Hail Mary to see if he could find a graceful way out of getting blood on his hands again.

The four other guys worked in tandem using hand signals and code words.

"I'm afraid your fate has already been sealed by a very hefty sum in my bank account. That was only a down payment of half with the rest after we have confirmed the kill. It sounds impersonal but we take this very seriously. We might even mourn your loss with a commemorative ceremony in your honor. I'm just kidding. You will be forgotten after the bullet leaves the chamber," Anson laughed purposely loud enough for his opponent to hear him mocking his existence.

The debate portion of their exchange had come to an end with nothing solved.

Bryce had a low threshold for pain but he was learning to push his understanding of what his body was capable of. Those things he had argued about with Quinn were going to be his saving grace.

"I wish we didn't have to do this. I know there's no avoiding what is going to happen next. Sometimes I feel like giving up. I've learned the hard way it's not in my blood. I would love a strong drink and maybe you can join me. We might find we have something in common. I have blood on my hands. If you're not careful yours is going to join the unlucky few. I'm not proud of it. What's done is done." He held the gun tightly wishing somehow Quinn was going to show up in the nick of time.

A twig snapped behind him making his blood run cold with the implication somebody was sneaking up on him.

8

Eight

The world was not what most people believed it to be. They were hiding in their homes unaware of the truth staring them in the face. There were fires everywhere metaphorical and otherwise ready to be put out. Enemies Foreign and domestic were plotting against those that took their freedoms seriously.

It was a bitter pill to swallow when they had to finally open up their eyes to the reality. Stories were being told based on real-life experiences. The news was where the truth could be glossed over with advertisements for products nobody needed.

Quinn didn't consider herself Teflon where nothing stuck to her. She was angry, but not at Niles Winthrop. Letting him into her head was what turned the tables in his favor.

It was one hundred and twenty-eight minutes of modern-day torture including depriving her of her senses. The bag over her head was nothing compared to water-boarding. She sputtered several times trying to take in enough oxygen when she was drowning every few seconds. It wasn't a simple story and hers was fraught with danger on every page until the bullet with her name finally found her.

The freezing cold water penetrating her lungs was forcing her to look for a reserve of strength. Shivering and convulsing was her body's answer to the invading force of the water being force-fed to her.

"I thought this was going to be easy. Hunting you was my favorite part and seeing the look in your eyes when I stood over top of you victorious was priceless. Nobody is going to know I had any part in this. I have sworn them to secrecy with the information being swept underneath the rug never to see the light of day again. I have the license to do whatever I want with you. I like some of the old favorites." He had already removed two of her fingernails and she didn't scream staring at him the entire time with hatred burning in a blaze of glory in her eyes.

"I would think you would know of all people this isn't going to work on me. Those missions were classified for a reason to protect the innocence. It's almost laughable when I hear myself say the words. The only people that it's protecting is military minds behind their cushy desks playing god with innocent lives." She thought of those photographs from her youth to make her laugh.

"At the risk of sounding like a broken record, I have better things to do than to spend time with you. You just finished saying you have no loyalty to them. What is stopping you from giving them the black eye they deserve by telling me what I want to know?" He put her through the torture of water boarding one more time to see if her lips would loosen under duress.

The way she thrashed and kicked against her bonds gave him a thrill beyond words. He thought about the offer to join him and was glad she declined. This wouldn't be happening had they been on the same side and he enjoyed seeing her resolve crumble. It wouldn't be long before she was broken, nothing more than a shell of what she once was.

Quinn held her breath but continued to thrash putting on a show worthy of an Oscar. She concentrated on those memories to make her smile. Separating her mind from her body was an art form not many people were able to do. She had found wisdom and sage advice from a monk in Tibet. Those lessons made it possible for her to slow down her breathing even while she was under extreme pressure.

She purposely kicked and pulled with the intention of breaking one of the straps holding her down to the chair. It felt like something was going to give and she hoped it wasn't going to be one of her bones. The wrist cuffs were cutting into her but the pain was nothing more than an aching nuisance in the back of her mind.

"I don't know why you are fighting so hard to hold onto those secrets. Most of them wouldn't spit on you if you were on fire. Don't you understand how you have been a tool for their amusement? I'm trying to put myself in your shoes without much luck," He responded before suddenly taking away the torture to give her room to breathe but his patience was wearing thin.

He brought the chair back up and watched her heave mouthfuls of water out of her mouth. There was damage being done. She wasn't going to last very much longer at this rate. He had to be careful to tread close to the edge without going over it. It was a balancing act and he was very good at keeping them breathing for as long as possible before finally extinguishing their last vestige of hope.

It was a cop-out to let her live beyond this moment. Normally, it would be his responsibility to send the message to end her suffering but he was front and center at the request of a man without a name. He knew it but most people didn't want to say it at the risk of incurring his wrath. His legend had grown until he was a monster underneath a child's bed while they were crying out for their mommy.

"It's a matter of principle and nothing to do with loyalty. Frankly, I don't want to give you the satisfaction of telling you a damn thing at the risk of making you happy. Don't worry, you are killing it when it comes to torture and I don't think I could've done better." She glared with her head pounding and her chest burning with the effort to breathe fresh oxygen while she still had the chance.

"That's high praise coming from you. Don't get me wrong, I do respect you, but this is business. I've been saving this for a special occasion." Mr. Rhodes made a big production out of looking through this big metal case until he pulled out this needle. "This is experimental and there's no telling what it's going to do to you." He came closer and was tapping the needle to show her the fluid about to enter into her bloodstream.

She bit down hard and could hear the cracking of her tooth. Her body convulsed with foam coming out of her mouth. She was wildly arching her chest with her eyes rolling into the back of her head.

The gagging caught his attention and he stared in stunned silence. It wasn't what he wanted and he was going to pay for letting it get this far. Bringing her in alive was paramount. This wasn't going to do and he was going to have to revive her by using extreme measures.

He frantically released her and turned his back to retrieve the lifesaving measures from the case. He exposed her chest and placed the paddles on her skin until they were fully charged. She wasn't moving until the electrical impulses radiated through her limbs. Mr. Rhodes was being deprived of seeing her beg for mercy and he wasn't going to settle for the next best thing.

"You're not going to die. Do you hear me? I will never hear the end of it. There's no telling what he will do when he finds out. I don't want to know the answer to that question. You need to fight and stop this insanity of trying to kill yourself." He believed in his heart this was the coward's way out and he couldn't understand how she had reached her breaking point.

He shocked her three more times before she started to breathe again with a steady rhythm on the monitors. The electrodes on her chest gave him the readings of her vitals minute by minute.

A breath of relief came out of his body. He bent over with the paddles charged and ready to go again. Something sparked inside of him and then he howled in pain when his leg buckled out from underneath him.

He placed his hands on the concrete floor with the paddles still gripped in his fingers.

Quinn had played her last card. It could've gone drastically wrong and the white light was a soothing reminder of what was waiting for her as a reward. She awakened with a blink of her eyes to see him make an error in judgment by turning his back on her. It was a calculated risk and it was going to pay off.

She had kicked him and reached over with her one free hand to press the button for the paddles to go off. Lifting her legs from the puddle of water formed in front of the chair was barely enough to prevent from electrocuting.

He grunted and groaned while she sat there fascinated, with her arms crossed over her knees. Mr. Rhodes was shaking and trembling. It didn't take long before he collapsed to the floor dead with one final breath.

"I didn't want any of this. It was supposed to be the other way around with you in this chair giving me the information I wanted. It's cold comfort to know that you will never be able to do this to another human being ever again. Mr. Rhodes, I finally know who you are and the fog has lifted on my memory. There was always that distant voice in the back of my mind." She had tuned him out and finally uncovered the hidden truth of his identity outside of Niles Winthrop.

Straining with every fiber of her being had her holding onto a scalpel. Cutting into the plastic cuffs was child's play. She shook her head when she noticed two of her fingernails missing in action. The pain was swimming upstream against the adrenaline.

It was by luck the water he had used to torture her had converged in a small dip in the floor where he was currently laying face down. Standing up on the chair was an effort when her legs felt like they were made of concrete.

"I would love to say this was fun but I hope never to do it again. Your secrets are going to die with you. I guess I'm going to have to find another way to find out what you know. Unfortunately, dead men tell no tales, but maybe something you are carrying will give me a clue." She was able to bridge the gap between the chair and where the machine for the paddles was located.

A well placed barefoot turned it off. She waited to make sure the electrical current was dead before making any untoward movements. Jumping down had her searching him to find his phone locked with a four-digit sequence, hard to crack but not impossible.

It would take time and that was a commodity she didn't have much of considering what was happening to Bryce. The phone was a work in progress but the slip of tangible paper with a name on it gave her a better idea of what they were facing.

It was time to call in a favor.

9

Nine

A pin could drop while Bryce was kneeling behind some branches when that twig snapped behind him. He spun to face the man. That mercenary had his hands raised with no visible weapon.

"You are one very lucky man. I had no idea what this was about and I wasn't concerned until I got a phone call. Quinn saved my life and the lives of my platoon. She has never asked for anything in return until now. You won't have any more problems from me and my men. Some things are bigger than money. Here is a set of keys to one of the vehicles out front. You'll find her about an hour away at the bus stop going east from this location," Anson offered and found him more than willing to take the win.

"I was ready to fight you but I'm glad I don't have to. I guess you were wrong about there being nothing to stop you from killing me. I know you don't feel very good about this. I guess I'm going to have to thank Quinn for getting me out of a sticky situation. I'm not saying I would've persevered. We might never be friends and that's okay with me. I can say with a degree of certainty you and your men wouldn't have gotten away unscathed." Bryce dangled the keys from his fingers and took his leave with the other men waiting for him to do something stupid.

"Get Quinn to tell you the story of how we met. I would suggest hearing it on an empty stomach. There is a special place in hell for some people and she sent them there to save us from a fate worse than death. We owe her our lives in more than one way. I thought she was dead. I should've known the good die young. She balances between what is right and wrong." Anson gave him a parting gift of a handshake.

It did surprise him to hear her voice. Smiling for the first time in a long time was courtesy of this weight being lifted from his shoulders. Something died in him when he heard of her passing and they did mourn with a commemorative ceremony in her honor.

Bryce found some clothing in the car. They were a little baggy but he wasn't going to look a gift horse in the mouth. He drove away with his eyes on the rearview mirror to check if they were in the process of pursuing him.

The knife in his pocket wasn't going to taste blood and he felt a little disappointed.

There were many milestones in somebody's life and this was going to be his. Something inside of him wanted desperately to prove to Quinn he was up to the task. The hunt was over for the time being. He suspected the end of the nightmare was far from over. He kept thinking about what started this chain of events and it all came back to him wanting to exact revenge.

It was tempting to turn around and go in the opposite direction. She deserved better than to have feelings for the man who had ripped the scab off of the metaphorical wound. It was misery to think that he could hurt her in that way but that was then and this was now. He brought the car to a standstill on the side of the road debating on letting her live her life without him.

It was wrong to drive back to her and jump into her arms. It might have been wrong but it felt right like they were two missing pieces to a puzzle. His heart was beating out of his chest from barely escaping the grim reaper's clammy hand on his shoulder.

He continued driving letting the time pass with hip hop music playing in the background. It became an anxious exercise knowing she was there in the darkness waiting for him to guide her into the light.

The bus stop was right there, after what felt like forever and she was sitting huddled inside the glass enclosure.

The door opened and she slipped into the passenger seat with barely a whisper.

"I don't want to hear it. The only thing I want to hear from you is gratitude. That was a huge marker I had to call in. I was never going to ask for anything. I feel bad I had to put him in the position but I would do it all over again. You mean the world to me, more than you will ever know. I've become a better person from knowing you." She was speaking to him without looking at him while he was driving.

"I can't thank you enough. I think I could've handled it but there's no way to know for certain. The numbers were certainly against me. It would've been an interesting fight. Any fight you can walk away from is a good one. Nobody had to fire the first shot and we went our separate ways with no harsh feelings." He saw this out of the way motel, and they were going to need some time to recharge after their ordeal.

The vacancy sign was blinking with the letter C burned out. He pulled into the parking lot and looked at her to see that she was shaking. Noticing she was missing two fingernails made him gasp. There was no telling what she had gone through and not one single word of her story had slipped from her lips.

"I need a hot bath and a warm body to join me under the covers when I'm done. You can help me scrub those hard to reach areas. Nothing is going to happen until after. I can say that but maybe there is a way to convince me. It's up to you to find out what that certain thing is to make me putty in your hands," She recalled and with vivid clarity found her memories of him touching her in just the right way, enough to bring the animal some relief inside of her.

He sprinted to the office and came back with a set of keys to the room at the far end of the parking lot. Using the key got them inside, it was refreshing to see clean sheets without anything skittering across the floor.

She braved the bathroom and turned on the light with bated breath. It was pristine with the white tub calling her name in a beckoning gesture with the hot water begging her to climb in until she was submerged. Turning the tap and watching the flow was bringing back painful memories of what she had just gone through.

Flashes of the insanity burned through her mind and she sighed with a deep breath fighting the urge to scream at the top of her lungs. She didn't break. It didn't mean that she wasn't close and she took the chance of him reviving her when she broke the tooth. It wasn't cyanide but it was a compound to stop her heart.

She stripped off the trench coat to assess the damages including her fingernails. There was a first-aid kit underneath the sink screwed into the wall. It was a process to open it up when her right hand was numb.

A masculine hand appeared and gently coaxed her to sit down on the edge of the tub.

Bryce applied the ointment and bandaged her two fingers. There were other cuts and bruises to attend to. Helping her into the tub had her leaning on him for support until she breathed deeply with the hot water surrounding her in a warm cocoon.

"He put me through hell. I went in there thinking it was going to go one way but it went another. Mr. Rhodes is no longer going to bother us. He's no longer going to bother anybody. I didn't get the answers I was looking for but I'm grateful to be able to help you. Thank you, for being kind and I hope you never lose the innocence from being with me." The water was soothing however the pain in her muscles was coming out in a profound way.

Bryce held her and used a washcloth with soap to help give her that moment of reprieve from the persistent danger. It wasn't sexual. He did enjoy her naked body dripping with water and it was causing a noticeable lump in his pants.

His hands massaged her shoulders and worked their way down to play her spine like a xylophone. Every little grunt and moan of response was music to his ears. He was finding pleasure in pleasing her. It was a slow journey with no pressure until she stepped from the tub and walked naked in front of him into the bedroom dripping with more than water.

10

Ten

It had been a long day, and lying down was just what the doctor ordered. Spreading her legs in invitation was her unconscious way to encourage the bad boy to come out of him. She was happy to see him breathing and wanted to capture another moment of physical pleasure in his arms.

Watching him undress slowly for her sexual amusement was the perfect spark to turn into a flame. His pants dropped with his underwear following suit to show the spring-loaded equipment in his possession.

Bryce moved forward with a clear drop of persuasion on the tip. Holding her head while she surveyed his endowment with a careful eye for detail was making him hungry to be consumed. She looked up at him and conveyed her wanton desire before parting her lips and delivering him to the oven of her mouth.

"We will always come back to one another. The stars have aligned to push us together. I couldn't stop thinking about you. It gave me that one thread to hold onto. I did something I'm not proud of. I killed myself in the hopes of being revived before it was irreversible. It was a plan but I know what they say about best-laid plans." She inhaled the head with this swirling motion to cause his legs to quiver in response.

He was praying this was forever and that she wouldn't find somebody new. There was no point in thinking about the worst-case scenario when she was holding his prized possession in a loving embrace. Her fingers trailed up and down the shaft with the vein down the back throbbing in her fist.

She loved how his body played perfectly into her dirty little fantasies. A little more pressure had him grunting and throwing his head back with the tendons of his neck pronounced. His number was up with the knob purposely and with forethought sliding in and out of her throat with ease.

"Those lips are like velvet and you have me exactly where you want me. I hope you don't take it too far before I get the chance to slip into you. I will say this is simply amazing. The way you seem to know what buttons to push has me at a loss for words." He was climbing to the summit with her lips gaining speed until her mouth was devouring the man and the animal at the same time inside of him.

She came up for air coating his link of sausage in the warm comfort of her mouth. It was plump and quite delicious with a creamy center begging to come out. Standing required holding onto his muscular arms for support. Draping her leg around his waist had his mushroom helmet kissing her lips.

"I can't stand it any longer. I want to feel you deep inside of me where you belong. Why do you have to be so damn irresistible? I need this to make me feel whole again. Give me that one thrust to take my breath away," She propositioned and received a healthy amount of meat buried to the hilt.

"I want you to know there is nothing I wouldn't do for you. This is nothing compared to the rest of your life with me. Practice will have me hitting all of those hot spots to make you yearn and crave those moments we find comfort in each other's arms." He felt at home and the growing pressure of pleasure had him swallowing hard while looking at the way his cock forced its way into the tight opening.

Glove like was an understatement. Her lips molded with liquid fire over his inches from the head to his balls. Thrusting was a slow and methodical effort to keep things from boiling over.

"I already do in ways I have never imagined. The pain is gone. I feel only the pleasure you give me." She yelped when her legs came out from underneath her and she landed softly on the mattress looking up at him.

He was still standing with her legs stretching to his shoulders and he burned inside every time she scratched his chest. The spectacle of throwing her hair back and forth on the pillow was sending signals to the little head. He fed her his enthusiasm bottoming out on each stroke. His pace was fueled by his excitement until he was grunting and falling down on top of her with his knees firmly planted in the mattress.

"I'm glad and being intimate with you is driving me crazy. My body craves to release the pleasurable buildup. I want to fire off my desire. You have your finger on the trigger and all you have to do is press a certain way to get my undivided attention." He found her enthusiasm and the way that her face morphed into a pleasing mask, quite contagious.

"Just give me the fire and make it burn," She moaned when the gates to her pleasure opened and closed repeatedly on the invading force of his tool drilling deep.

Her heels began pounding against him and then her body lifted with a deafening scream to signal the moment of truth was upon her. Her lower half was suspended with his hands underneath to keep her from releasing her grip on the heat of his arousal. She was frozen with every muscle rippling waiting for him to join her.

He held her firmly and drove with precision until he could see the light. It flashed with brilliance in her eyes and he gave her the sizzling reminder of how he felt for her. Deliciously exhausted was a good way to describe how they felt when the dust settled.

She languished in his arms smelling his aftershave and trailing her fingers down over his body to feel him squirm underneath her touch. The passion had been temporarily satiated. It was only a matter of time before they were at it again. She could already feel a resurgence of energy burning within her loins.

Jumping on top of him and starting things all over again was a pleasure she couldn't contain. Riding back and forth on top of him was rubbing him the right way to bring his flag to full mast. His love pole became her sexual toy with him lying on the mattress at her mercy. They moved from one position to another until they were on the floor, out of breath with their energy depleted.

They stuck together with the smell of sex in the air.

"You're going to kill me, but I will die with a happy smile on my face. I can just imagine what the chalk outline of my body would look like," Bryce stated with his arm around her and her head on his chest.

It wasn't long before they were asleep in each other's arms.

~

A few hours later and they finally walked out under the cover of darkness. There was an explosion and the car incinerated with pieces of metal flying everywhere. Windows in the motel were broken in the aftermath with the fire scorching the siding with telltale black marks.

A television set over a fireplace had one man's full attention. The volume was turned up and he sat at the edge of his seat. He was watching with his lips dry and cracked with the taste of revenge in his mouth.

"This reporter has been at the scene for the past hour. The police cannot confirm or deny there was an explosion. There are two casualties with one fatality. A man was taken away to the morgue. There was a woman and she is in critical condition not expected to make it through the night. On another note, Mr. Rhodes was found dead in his hotel room apparently of a heart attack..." The man was smoking a cigar and drinking warm apple cider while staring blankly at the screen.

"You're not going to get away from me that easily. I've taken the one thing you love and now I'm going to take your life. I will be the last face you see." He looked down at his itinerary and slipped from his chair into a standing position.

He grabbed his coat and walked out clutching a picture of Quinn in his fist.

Subscribe Now For Exclusive Content!

Stay In Touch With LT To Receive Book Updates and Offers!

Sign up for my newsletter HERE
You can also join our ARC team HERE

Get in touch with L.T. by email at LTGrundyBooks@gmail.com

Subscribe now for exclusive updates, promos, giveaways, and updates on the next book!

A Note To You, The Reader

P.S. Readers:

Thank you so much for taking the time to read my book. Your feedback is very important to me. I'd like to ask a small favor. Would you be so kind as to click HERE and leave me an **HONEST** review?

Thank you so much!

Stay awesome,

L.T. Grundy

About the Author

L.T. Grundy lives with the love of his life Mary. They are the proud parents of two St. Bernards, Bella and Bastian. L.T and Mary enjoy outdoor activities like hiking and fishing, and anything else where the pups can tag along! Visit our Facebook page where you can connect with L.T.and sign up for our newsletter to receive offers and updates on when the next book will be released!

Also by L.T. Grundy

BLOOD IN THE EYE OF THE STORM
L.T. GRUNDY

TRAPPED BY THE BLOOD
L.T. GRUNDY

BLOOD RELEVATION
L. T. GRUNDY

www.ingramcontent.com/pod-product-compliance
Lightning Source LLC
LaVergne TN
LVHW050344160826
845677LV00014B/3777

* 9 7 9 8 3 7 4 0 0 4 7 6 2 *